Leonard Kessler

SUPER BOWL

Greenwillow
Read-alone

GREENWILLOW BOOKS • New York

FOR ETHEL,
SUPER FRIEND

First Edition   10 9 8 7 6 5 4 3 2 1

Library of Congress Cataloging in Publication Data
Kessler, Leonard P (date)   Super Bowl.
(A Greenwillow read-alone book)
Summary: The Animal Champs play the Super Birds
in the football Super Bowl, and the losers console
themselves that there is another year coming.
[1. Football–Fiction. 2. Animals–Fiction]
I. Title.   PZ7.K484Su   [E]   80-10171
ISBN 0-688-80270-2   ISBN 0-688-84270-4 lib. bdg.

Contents

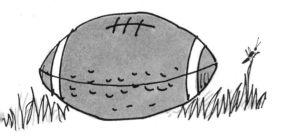

The Teams

WORM
CHEER LEADER

TURTLE

FROG

DOG
(PLAYER-COACH)

RABBIT

RACCOON

CAT

The Cheers

FOOTBALL
FOOTBALL
Lots of fun.
Super Birds
Super Birds
Number One!

Birds can run.
Birds can fly.
Birds can make
Animal Champs cry!

BOO! HOO!
BOO! HOO!
Booooooooooo!

SUPER BIRDS

Duck Duck
Runs like a truck!

Two four six eight
The Animal Champs
are oh so great!

Hit them high.
Hit them low.
Tackle Goose.
Tackle Crow.
Yea, Champs...Let's go!

ANIMAL CHAMPS

7

1. One Week to Go

"One more week before the
big game," said Frog.
"It's the Super Bowl game,"
said Raccoon.
"We play the Super Birds,"
said Cat.

"We are the Animal Champs,"
Turtle said.

"We are number one!"
said Rabbit.

"Yea, Animal Champs!"
Worm cheered.

"One week to go,"
said Duck and Goose.
"We are the Super Birds,"
said Gull and Owl.

"We are number one,"
yelled Chicken and Crow.
"Yea, Super Birds,"
the little birds cheered.

The next day the Animal Champs
worked on a secret play.
"Remember, when I yell
HOP, HOP, HOP,
the next play will be our
secret play," Dog told Frog.

The Super Birds
worked on new plays too.

"Hold it! Hold it!" Owl shouted.

"Where is Duck?"

"Duck is late," said Gull.

"She is always late," Crow said.

"I'm here! I'm here!" yelled Duck.

"My alarm clock did not go off."

"Buy a new clock," Owl told her.

The next day Duck was late again.

"I forgot to buy a new clock,"
Duck said.

"I'll remember tomorrow."

But Duck did not remember.

She was late again.

"You will be sorry," said Chicken.

"Super Bowl winners

work out every day.

You are not in good shape."

2. The Big Game

"It's Super Bowl Day," shouted Frog.

"Everybody is here!" said Goose.

"Where is Duck?" yelled Owl.

"Late again," said Crow.

"I'm here. I'm here. I went to buy
a new clock," said Duck.

"You are just in time for the kickoff,"
Chicken said.

The Animal Champs kicked the ball.

Up, up it went.

Chicken got the ball.

She ran with the ball.

Frog and Dog tackled her.

"First down and ten yards
   to go," said Fox, the referee.

The Super Birds went into a huddle.

"Give the ball to me.

They can't stop me," said Duck.

The teams lined up.

Owl shouted, "Hup one.

Hup two. Hup. Hup."

Chicken gave the ball to Duck.

"I'm running for a touchdown,"
Duck yelled.

"Oh NO! Duck!" shouted Crow.

"What's the matter?"
Duck shouted back.

"The football! You dropped it
on the forty yard line!" yelled Crow.

Cat fell on the ball.

"Animals' ball. First down,"
said Fox.

"Duck, Duck.
Runs like a truck.
Yea, Animal Champs,"

Worm cheered.

The Animal Champs
went into a huddle.
"Let's give them our
   razzle dazzle play," Dog said.
"The secret play?" asked Frog.
"No! Not the secret play,"
   whispered Dog.
"Not till I say HOP HOP HOP."

Dog got the ball.

He gave the ball to Raccoon.

Raccoon tossed it to Cat.

Cat flipped the ball to Rabbit.

Rabbit ran past Turtle.

"Rabbit has the ball,"
shouted Duck.
"Tackle him. Tackle him."
All the birds tackled Rabbit.
But Rabbit did not have the ball.
Who had the ball?

It was Turtle!

Turtle ran into the end zone.
"It's a touchdown,"
yelled Frog.

"Yea, Turtle!" Worm cheered.

"Yea for me!" cheered Turtle.

Dog gave Turtle a big hug.

"You were great!" said Frog.

Rabbit kicked the extra point.

The Animal Champs kicked the ball
to the Super Birds.
"First and ten for the Super Birds,"
said Fox.

Owl got the ball. Back she went.

"Watch that Gull!" Cat told Frog.

"Looks like a short pass,"
said Dog.

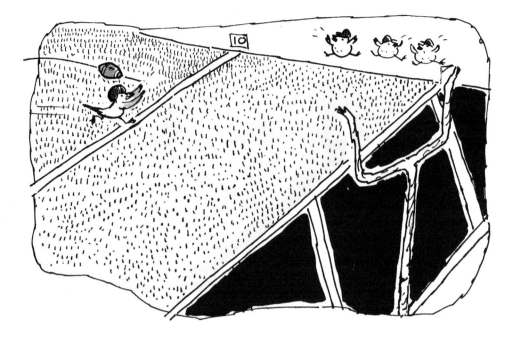

But it was not a short pass.

It was a long pass to Gull.

He caught the ball

on the ten yard line.

He ran across the goal line.

"Touchdown! Touchdown!"
the Birds cheered.

"I told you to watch that Gull,"
said Cat.

"Gull? I thought you said *girl!*"
Frog smiled.

Crow kicked the extra point.

It was the end of the first half.

The score was

"We must play better," said Owl.

"I'm tired," said Duck.

"You are not in good shape,"
Chicken said.

"You always came late,"
Goose told her.

"Let's not fight. Let's win
this game," said Crow.

3. Second Half

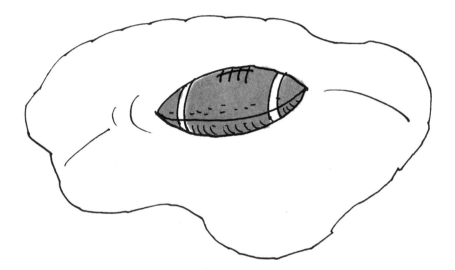

The Super Birds kicked off
to the Animal Champs.
But the Animal Champs
did not make a first down.
The ball went back
to the Super Birds.

Owl told Goose, "On the next play,
I will hit you with a long pass."

Goose ran down the field.
"Hit me! Hit me!" she yelled.

POW! Turtle hit Goose.

"Ten yards for hitting," said Fox.

Goose kicked Turtle.

"OUCH!" Goose cried.

"I broke my foot."

"Never kick a turtle," said Owl.

"Ten yards for kicking!"

called Fox.

"Second down and ten."

Duck ran down the sideline.
She had the ball.
"They won't stop me this time,"
she said.
"Look out for the water bucket,"
yelled Crow.

But Duck did not hear her.
She did not see the bucket
on the sideline.

Duck stepped right into the bucket.

It flew up in the air

and fell on top of her head.

PLOP!

Duck dropped the ball.

Dog fell on top of the ball.

Fox blew the whistle.

"Two minutes to go.

Time out," he said.

The score was still

Animal Champs	7
Super Birds	7

Frog hopped over to Dog.

"Now?" she asked.

"NOW!" Dog said.

Frog smiled.

The Animals came out
of their huddle.
Dog shouted, "HOP HOP!"
Raccoon snapped the ball
to Dog. Back, back he went.

Frog hopped down the field.

She crossed the goal line.

"Duck, Duck! Watch Frog!"

Owl screamed.

But it was too late.

Duck did not get there in time.

Dog threw a long pass.

Frog hopped high, high in the air.

"Frog has it!" yelled Rabbit.

"Touchdown!" Fox said.

"Six points," Cat shouted.

Rabbit kicked the extra point.

The gun went off. BANG!

The game was over.

The score was

Animal Champs 14
Super Birds 7

"We are number one!"

Worm shouted.

"We are number one!"

the Animal Champs all yelled.

"Well, we are number two,"

said Goose.

Duck sat on the bench.

She held her head.

She was very sad.

"I lost the game," said Duck.

"No. I lost the game.

I kicked Turtle.

I did not play very well,"

Goose said.

"We *all* lost the game.
We did not play
like Super Birds,"
said Gull.

"But there will be
a Super Bowl next year,"
said Owl.
"And we will play better,"
said Chicken.

Duck jumped up
from the bench.
"Hey, Animal Champs!"
she shouted.
"WAIT TILL NEXT YEAR!"

"WAIT
TILL
NEXT
YEAR!"

all the Super Birds shouted.

SUPER BOWL
SUPER BOWL
WHAT A GAME!
WHO WAS THE HERO?

Frog

That's his name!

LEONARD KESSLER is a popular writer and illustrator of children's books. He is best known for his sports I Can Read Books–*Here Comes the Strikeout; Kick, Pass and Run;* and *On Your Mark, Get Set, Go.* He is also the illustrator of *I Was Thinking,* a book of poems by Freya Littledale.

Mr. Kessler was born in Ohio and grew up in Pittsburgh. He was graduated from Carnegie Institute of Technology with a degree in Fine Arts, Painting and Design. He lives in New City, Rockland County, New York.